BATTER UP!

Written and photographed
by Neil Johnson

SCHOLASTIC INC.

New York Toronto London Auckland Sydney

To the stouthearted men, past and present, of the Second Tuesday Team and to those glorious nights when the laughter was loudest.

Special thanks to the 1989 Sunset Acres Indians:

Jason, Kerry, Patrick, Clay, Brad, B.J., Brandon, Cedric, Chad, Darrell, and Steve. Thanks also to the coaches: Carlin, Dottie, and Patrick.

One! Two! Three! — SUNSET!!!

ISBN 0-590-42730-X
Copyright © 1990 by Neil Johnson.
All rights reserved. Published by Scholastic Inc.

12 11 10 9 8 7 6 5 4 3 2 1   7   0 1 2 3 4 5/9

BATTER UP!

"Batter up!" the umpire shouted.

Taking a deep breath, Nick slowly walked out to the white rectangle in the dirt behind home plate. He swung his bat for practice. Once. Twice.

Focusing his eyes on the pitcher, Nick gripped the bat tightly and felt its weight one more time. He cocked the bat behind him and felt his heart beating wildly. He studied the ball in the pitcher's hand.

The chatter from the field and the friendly advice from the dugout slowly faded as he concentrated.

This time he was ready!

It had been less than a year ago when Nick had gone out to watch Peter, his new friend from school, play in a baseball game.

Nick sat on the bleachers with the parents, brothers, and sisters of the players wondering why he was the only ten-year-old not taking part in the excitement on the field. The Indians looked great in their bright yellow uniforms.

After the game, Peter found Nick. "What did you think, Nick? Are you coming out for the team next year?"

Nick was doubtful. "I've never played on a team before. You sure they'd let me on?"

"No problem!" Peter grinned. "You'll get on."

The next spring came quickly. Nick borrowed a glove and went out to meet Peter to begin getting his arm in shape by playing catch.

"What has eighteen legs and catches flies?" Peter's face was serious.

"I don't know," Nick replied. "Some kind of spider?"

"Are you kidding?" Peter laughed. "A baseball team! A BASEBALL TEAM!"

"OK, OK! I get it." Nick smiled.

Peter had started playing with the Indians four years ago. Back then they played "T" ball. There was no pitcher. The young players batted the ball off a stand called a "T". Now the Indians played official league baseball. Peter was the pitcher and he knew a lot about baseball.

"Your glove is really important!" Peter told him. "Your glove should be a part of you— like a big hand."

"Oh, yeah?" Nick grinned. "What about when you're batting?"

Peter began laughing again and asked Nick when the last time was that he'd seen a spider wearing baseball cleats.

For a couple of weeks, every day after school they threw the baseball back and forth, until Nick thought he could actually throw the ball a pretty good distance.

The Indians' first practice came on a warm spring afternoon. The clover was thick on the field, and a breeze was blowing under the clear blue sky. Coach Andy was unloading the bats, balls, and batting helmets behind the backstop when Nick and Peter arrived on their bikes.

When everybody had arrived, they ran one lap around the field to loosen up. The three coaches, Andy, Chuck, and Richard, called everybody together to meet Nick. Then they split the players up for outfield and infield practice.

Nick went with the outfield group, where Coach Chuck batted them grounders and fly balls. Nick was glad he and Peter had been practicing.

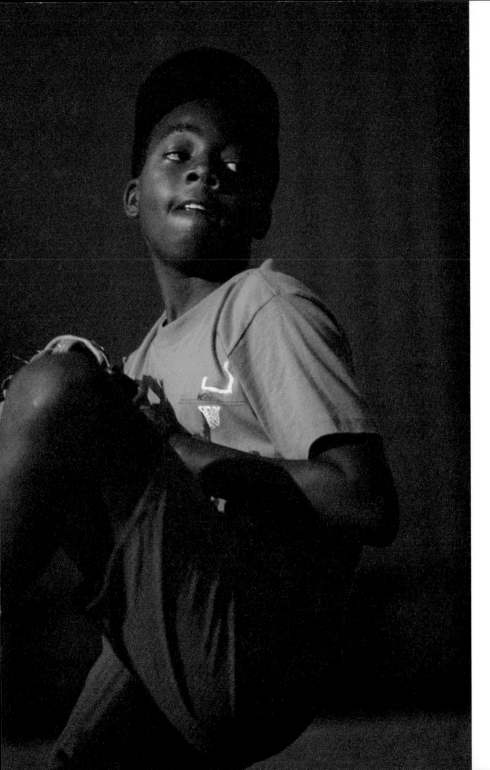

Coach Chuck batted the ball way up into the air. Several times the ball hit the ground behind Nick. Trying to catch those almost made him fall over backwards. He learned that he had to judge the flight of the ball quickly, get a bit behind where it was going to land, and then move forward to catch it.

"Stay in front of the ball coming toward you," called Coach Chuck. "If you can't get it in your glove, block it with your body—especially a grounder. Just don't let it get past you."

A fast ground ball skipped off a bump in the field and barely missed Nick's face. It nearly scared him to death.

Coach Richard took Peter a little ways off to help him practice pitching.

Coach Andy batted the ball one-handed around the field, giving
instructions about where the ball was to be thrown. Go to first! Go
to third, then second! Go to second, then first! Fire it home!

"Now run it in." Coach Andy hit the ball to each player who then
dashed in to home, flipping the ball to the catcher. Nick ran as
hard as he could. If there was one thing he could do as well as the
others, it was run.

Batting practice nearly wore Nick out his first time. The balls kept coming at him, and he kept swinging, but the best he could do was hit foul balls way to his left or dribblers into the infield.

Coach Richard gave him a lighter bat and showed him a way to place his feet that would keep him from fouling the ball so much. "Now, keep your eye on the ball all the way in," said Coach Richard.

Finally Nick felt his bat connect solidly with a pitch. Peter shouted, "All right, Nick! Good hit!"

The next day before practice, the team met at the Sunset clubhouse to get their uniforms. "Here, Nick." Coach Andy tossed him a jersey, pants, and a cap. "If these fit, you're number forty. Remember, these are just for games."

Wow! thought Nick. My own uniform! Now he really felt like part of the team.

The Indians practiced several times after school each week for a month. As the season got closer, the team felt better. They had learned about batting, forcing runners out, cutting runners off, stealing bases, and backing up other players on the field for times when someone missed the ball. But every single player still made errors. Sometimes they let grounders zip through their legs, or made wild throws that were too high or too wide for anyone to catch.

Nick learned that some days were much better than others. During one batting practice, he hit the ball solidly out of the infield three times. But the very next day, he must have had thirty strikes. Nick decided that batting was the hardest part of baseball.

At the end of one practice, Coach Andy sat everyone down in the grass behind the backstop and said, "OK, now everyone listen up and listen up good. We've got our first game this coming Thursday night, and you'll be out there playing—not practicing."

He looked each of the players in the eye. "I know you can play ball now. I've seen you do it. If you play hard and think about what you're doing, we'll win that game. Now everyone go on home and think baseball. I'll see you Thursday at seven P.M. sharp."

Nick was the first player at the field, but the others showed up soon afterwards. They all wore their bright yellow uniforms.

Nick felt like he had a zillion excited butterflies in his stomach.

Even Coach Andy was nervous. He got everyone together and gave them what seemed like every piece of advice he had ever given.

"And remember, let's play as a team. If someone messes up, tell 'em it's OK—to shake it off. And if someone makes a good play, tell 'em so. Oh, and one more thing…"

Nick had heard most of what Coach Andy said before at practice. It was hard to concentrate now.

When it was time to begin the game, Coach Andy got the Indians together in the dugout and led them in a pre-game cheer: "One! Two! Three! SUNSET!!!"

The Indians took the field at a run to the cheers and applause of all the parents, brothers, and sisters in the bleachers. Nick knew where his mom and dad were sitting, but after waving to them, he tried to keep from looking back at the crowd. He had to concentrate on his job.

Nick was put in left field. Peter was on the pitcher's mound. The batter looked a long way off.

"H-e-e-e-y, batter-batter-batter, SWING!" Nick called with the others. He half expected the first batter to hit the ball right over his head, but Nick was relieved when Peter struck the first batter out.

The next guy hit two fouls and then missed a pitch completely. Out! The third batter hit an easy grounder to the shortstop, who tossed it to first for the third out. The Indian dugout filled quickly. They talked excitedly about who was up and in what order. Peter was first up. He grabbed a bat and ran out to the plate.

Nick's first turn at bat wasn't as bad as he had figured. He watched the ball streak by. "ST-E-E-E-RIKE!" the umpire called. Nick gulped and glanced back at Coach Andy, who was standing near third base calling advice to each batter.

"Good cut, Nick! That one didn't have your name on it!" he yelled. "Wait on a good pitch and swing straight!"

It really wasn't all that different from batting practice, except that his heart pounded a lot harder and there was much more noise. But those things made a big difference. He let three bad pitches go by and swung and missed another pitch completely. But the pitcher threw a fourth pitch that didn't go right over the plate in the strike zone.

"Ball four!" the ump said. "Take your base, son."

Coach Richard, standing beside first base, slapped Nick on the back as he trotted up to the base. "Good eye, Nick! Way to watch 'em!"

That made him feel good, but Nick wasn't so sure it was really his eye that had gotten him to first base. It seemed more like four bad pitches.

The next batter was the Indians' third out, which meant Nick had to leave first base, get his glove, and head back onto the field.

Later in the game, Nick was walked to first base again. But this time the catcher dropped a pitch, and Coach Richard sent him as fast as he could run to second base. Nick slid safely to the base before the catcher could throw the ball to cut him off.

"All right, Nick! Good steal!" the Indians cheered from the dugout. Nick just grinned back at them. He was forced out at third base, though, and didn't get on base again the rest of the game.

Every once in a while, Coach Andy would change players
around to let them get the feel of another position. Nick got to play
third base once.

While at third, he had a hard grounder hit right at him. In the
split second before the ball got to him, Nick closed his eyes. The
next thing he knew, the ball had scooted right between his legs.
The batter made it to Nick at third base.

A triple caused by Nick's error!

But the triple wasn't the worst. The Indians were playing the
Tigers next, and it was an important game.

Nick's team had not yet lost a game, but everyone said the
Tigers were tough.

The next evening, at the field, Nick watched the other team
warming up. Yes, they were good, all right. The way they tossed the
ball back and forth so easily showed that they had probably been
practicing for months. And they had three players taller than the
tallest guy on Nick's team.

Then Nick noticed something unusual about one of the other
players. She was a girl! They had a girl on their team!

The game was close. First the Indians scored two runs. Then the Tigers scored three. It was really exciting. In the dugout, when an Indian got a hit, the other Indians would climb the chainlink fence in their excitement. The score was soon tied at 8–8. The umpires were the only people there not getting hoarse from yelling and cheering.

In his left field position, Nick had caught one fly ball, and had stopped one good grounder. Later, he had helped get a runner out by making a good throw to third base. He had watched the girl strike out three times.

Now, when she stepped up to the plate, Nick moved in closer toward the infield just in case.

Peter let go a pitch.

CRACK! The ball climbed up and toward Nick. But it was too late! He had moved up too far! Nick backed up faster and faster to get under the ball. No! He tripped, landing in a twisted pile of legs and arms in the grass. He heard the ball plop onto the ground behind him. He couldn't believe this was happening!

It only took seconds, but it seemed like forever. Nick watched as the center fielder ran back to the fence to get the ball and heave it toward the infield. But it was too late. She was rounding third and heading for home. The wild cheering from the Tigers' dugout and bleachers was thunderous.

The Indians lost the game—9–8.

Peter and Nick threw the ball back and forth silently the next day before practice. Nick had not wanted to come today, but Peter had even insisted on their going early.

"Come on, Nick," Peter finally said. "We've all messed up. Everybody on the team. Robert dropped that easy right field pop-up in the second game. Clay missed third base with his foot when he was trying for that home run. And remember when Frankie stole second that time he forgot Louis was already on second! Boy, was Frankie embarrassed! And I walked *eight* guys in a row in one inning once. Remember? But you still see us out there, don't you?"

"Yes, I guess," Nick admitted.

"Well, OK, then!" Peter smiled. "We all feel bad when we mess up, but baseball and especially our team are too much fun to just give up on."

They continued to throw until Frankie came up. "Hey, Nick," he said, pounding him on the back. "That was a great throw you made to Mike yesterday!" Nick remembered the throw and thanked Frankie.

When Clay, Robert, and Louis arrived, they said, "Hi, Nick," just like always. They were laughing and joking like nothing had happened the day before.

When Coach Andy arrived, he dumped the equipment bag out behind the backstop and called everyone over.

"OK, guys," he said. "The season is almost over and you're all doing great, despite what the Tigers did to us yesterday. I'm proud to be coaching this team."

Then he looked straight at Nick. "I'm proud of each and every one of you, whether we win or lose. And, you know, if we keep playing our best we could still be in the championship playoffs."

"OK, is everyone warmed up? Everyone take a lap around the field and we'll get started. I want to work on bunting today."

That was all in the past now. The Indians
had made it to the playoffs and now they
were facing the Tigers again.

This time Nick was ready.
He wanted a hit so badly he could taste it.

Coach Andy kept giving advice from his left. Nick watched a
strike and two balls go by. On the next pitch, when the ball left the
pitcher's hand it seemed to be coming in right over the plate.
It was a perfect pitch.

The ball never made it to the catcher's glove.

Nick swung the bat around hard and sure. The impact of the ball hitting the bat vibrated instantly all the way down Nick's body to his toes as he twisted around in the follow-through. Out of the corner of his eye, he saw the ball flying right between the third baseman and the shortstop. They were not going to touch it.

But Nick didn't watch the ball. He dropped the bat, set his eyes on first base, and took off running. He ran faster, he thought, than he had ever run before!